Pencilmate vs. Pencil

A Pencilmation STORY

by Steve Behling
illustrated by JJ Harrison

PENGUIN YOUNG READERS LICENSES
AN IMPRINT OF PENGUIN RANDOM HOUSE LLC, NEW YORK

FIRST PUBLISHED IN THE UNITED STATES OF AMERICA
BY PENGUIN YOUNG READERS LICENSES, AN IMPRINT OF
PENGUIN RANDOM HOUSE LLC, NEW YORK, 2023

VISIT US ONLINE AT PENGUINRANDOMHOUSE.COM.

MANUFACTURED IN CHINA

ISBN 9780593659106   10 9 8 7 6 5 4 3 2 1 TOPL

DESIGN BY TAYLOR ABATIELL

CHAPTER ONE

"This is going to be the best day ever!"
Pencilmate shouted as loud as he possibly could.
He had just woken up and was still in bed. He
couldn't wait to get up and find something
completely awesome to do.

Pencilmate glanced over at his bedroom
window and saw the Sun just peeking out over
the horizon.

"Good morning, Sun!" Pencilmate hollered at
the top of his voice. "You're looking extra sunny
today!"

There came a low rumbling noise from the
sky, and a booming voice said, "You're too loud,

Pencilmate!" That was the Sun, and it covered its ears.

"Sorry, Sun!" Pencilmate apologized. "I'll try to be quiet. I mean, as quiet as a guy can be who's about to have the best day ever!"

"Good luck with that," the Sun replied.

Suddenly, Pencilmate heard his stomach rumble loudly.

GURRRRRRRRGLE!

"Boy, am I hungry!" he said. "I'll just jump out of bed and fix myself the world's largest stack of pancakes for breakfast!"

And so Pencilmate hopped out of bed, ready to face the day, when there was a big *SPLASH!*

"What the—something's not right!" Pencilmate exclaimed as he found himself bobbing up and down. He looked around and saw that his bedroom was completely flooded with water!

Well, this is definitely not normal, he

thought as he tried to keep afloat. *Did I leave a faucet running overnight?*

That seemed kind of silly, but sillier stuff had a way of happening to Pencilmate all the time.

So he was only a *little* surprised when he felt something move past his legs.

"Uh-oh," Pencilmate said.

A second later, a big, green, lizard-like head poked out from the water. It was a sea monster! The creature spewed a mouthful of water right in Pencilmate's face.

"Ack!" Pencilmate said. "Go away, I'm not thirsty! Also, I'm not sea monster food!"

The sea monster ducked back under the water and then reappeared a short distance away. It started to come for Pencilmate, so he swam as fast as he could back to the safety of his bed. Scrambling on top of the blankets, he watched as the sea monster stopped short and sunk back below the water's surface.

"Seriously, how did that thing get in my room?" Pencilmate asked. "My landlord has a strict 'no pets' policy!"

And then, he realized that there was only one possible explanation.

No, it wasn't because the Sun was so angry at him for being loud that it decided to flood

Pencilmate's room and put a sea monster in there to spit in his face.

It was . . .

"Pencil!!!" Pencilmate thundered.

His eyes shot up toward the ceiling, and then Pencilmate saw it.

A big yellow pencil was just hanging there above him! For whatever reason, Pencil always wanted to mess with Pencilmate. With a few quick strokes, Pencil could turn any situation into a complete nightmare. Or, in this case, turn Pencilmate's bedroom into an ocean with one big, annoying sea monster.

"Pencil, Pencil, PENCIL!" Pencilmate said, shaking an angry fist. "It's always you, isn't it?"

Pencil nodded up and down as if it were agreeing with him. See, the thing about Pencil was that it never said a word. Pencil just did stuff that drove Pencilmate up a wall.

"You're always causing trouble! Well, I've had enough of your . . . of your . . . ," Pencilmate said, struggling to find the right word.

Suddenly, Pencil wrote the word "SHENANIGANS" on the wall.

"No, not 'shenanigans,'" Pencilmate said.

Then Pencil wrote, "HIJINKS?"

"Yes!" Pencilmate hollered. "Hijinks! I've had enough of your hijinks! And this time, I'm gonna do something about it!"

Pencilmate reached for his phone sitting on the night table floating next to his bed. But just as he was about to grab it, the sea monster popped up from the water and ate it.

BUUUUUURP!

"Oh, come on," Pencilmate said. "That was a new phone!"

Thinking fast, Pencilmate opened the night-table drawer and pulled out a pen, several sheets of paper, some envelopes, and postage stamps. Then he quickly wrote some letters, stuffed them inside the envelopes, addressed them, and slapped on the stamps.

Reaching inside the drawer again, Pencilmate pulled out a long wooden oar and began paddling his bed out of the room to the front yard, which was also flooded.

Pencilmate rowed the bed over to his mailbox and put the letters inside. He raised the flag to let the mail person know that there was mail ready to be picked up.

Almost instantly, the mail person showed up in a motorboat, opened the mailbox, and took the letters with a tip of their cap.

Pencilmate sat there on his bed and rolled his eyes up at the sky, whistling for a minute. He saw the Sun and noticed that it was wearing earplugs. At least Pencilmate wouldn't have to worry about making so much noise now.

Not even a minute passed before an even BIGGER motorboat arrived at Pencilmate's house, and out jumped his friends Pencilmiss, Big Guy, and Mini-Pencilmate!

"What took you so long?" Pencilmate said.

"Sorry," Pencilmiss replied. "We had to build the motorboat, or we would have been here sooner."

"So, you need our help?" Big Guy asked.

"Do I ever!" Pencilmate said. "And I'll tell you all about it, just as soon as the person reading this book turns the page."

(Pssst . . . This would be a good time to turn the page.)

CHAPTER TWO

As they went inside the house, Pencilmate rowed over to the bathroom and pulled the drain on the bathtub. All the water inside the house— and outside, too—quickly drained out.

"Huh," Pencilmate said. "I should have thought of that sooner."

Heading into the kitchen, Pencilmate saw his friends had already gathered around the table, the motorboat parked right next to them. Pencilmiss sat there patiently while Big Guy ate directly out of a big box of Collect All the Winged Horses cereal. Mini-Pencilmate jumped up and down on the table excitedly, pointing at a burst on the box that said "Free Toy Surprise Inside!"

"I'm glad you could all make it here today," Pencilmate said.

CRUNCH.

"Because I've got a real problem, and I need your help," Pencilmate continued.

CRUNCH CRUNCH CRUNCH.

"You see, it's about Pencil—"

CRUNCHITY CRUNCH.

"—and it's—"

CRUUUUUUUUNCH.

"WHAT?" Pencilmiss said, unable to hear anything over the sound of Big Guy's eating.

"I said—"

CRUNCH CRUNCH CRUNCH CRUNCH CRUNCH CRUNCH—

"Maybe you should wait until Big Guy's done eating," Pencilmiss suggested.

Pencilmate rolled his eyes but decided that Pencilmiss was probably right (which she pretty much always was), and so he just sat there as Big Guy munched his way through the cereal.

After what seemed like an entire day had

passed, the munching was nearly over.

"I think he's almost reached the bottom of the box," Pencilmiss said hopefully.

Just as Pencilmate was about to speak, Pencil appeared once again. It drew an even bigger box of Collect All the Winged Horses cereal!

Pencilmate glared at Pencil, while Mini-Pencilmate, overjoyed at the prospect of getting an even bigger toy surprise, went wild. Big Guy dug into the box with gusto, his head disappearing inside as he ate with abandon.

CRUNCH CRUNCH CRUNCH CRUNCH!

The big box of cereal teetered back and forth on the table as Big Guy now climbed *inside* the giant box, eating the cereal in pursuit of the prize for Mini-Pencilmate.

"See, this is exactly the kind of thing I'm talking about!" Pencilmate complained. "Do you see how that thing's always messing with me?"

Pencilmiss nodded. "Yeah, but what can we do about it?"

"Well . . . something, that's for sure!" Pencilmate yelled over the sound of crunching. "Pencil just makes me so angry!"

"It's like it knows exactly what will annoy you," Pencilmiss added. "Like it knows all your weaknesses."

As the crunching continued and the enormous box of cereal atop the table continued to teeter, inspiration struck Pencilmate.

"That's it!" Pencilmate said. "What if we find Pencil's weakness? Maybe then we could finally stop it from bugging me once and for all!"

"Um, Pencilmate?" Pencilmiss said as she backed away from the wobbling box. "You might want to—"

"Not now, Pencilmiss! I'm making ideas inside my head!" Pencilmate replied. "That's where the best ideas come from, by the way."

"Yeah, but—" Pencilmiss said.

Pencilmate rubbed his hands in excitement as his brain began thinking of how they might discover Pencil's weakness.

Unfortunately for Pencilmate, he didn't heed Pencilmiss's warnings, and the giant box of Collect All the Winged Horses cereal fell over, flattening Pencilmate beneath it.

A moment later, Big Guy emerged from the box, holding up a huge toy winged horse.

"I found it," Big Guy said before letting out a noisy *BURRRRRRRP*. "It has 'flapping-wing action.'"

Squealing with delight, Mini-Pencilmate clapped his hands together. He was overjoyed!

Pencilmate, not so much.

CHAPTER THREE

Aside from waking up in a flooded home, getting attacked by a sea monster, having his phone eaten by said sea monster, and being crushed by a giant box of Collect All the Winged Horses cereal, it was shaping up to be a pretty good day for Pencilmate.

You know, except for the "good day" part.

"All right, everybody, get ready for Mission: Im-*Pencil*-able!" Pencilmate said.

Pencilmiss gave Pencilmate a funny look.

"'Mission Im-*Pencil*-able'?" she said. "I'm not sure that works."

"Yeah, I don't get it," Big Guy mumbled.

"Look, what we call the mission isn't important," Pencilmate said. "It's what we do on the mission that really counts. And that's finding Pencil's weakness!"

"Which is . . . what, exactly?" Pencilmiss asked. "Anyone have any ideas?"

Then Big Guy began waving his hand excitedly.

"Yes, Big Guy?" Pencilmate said. "What's your idea?"

"I don't have an idea," Big Guy said. "I just felt like waving my hand."

"Oh," Pencilmate sighed. He shrugged his shoulders and said, "Anyway, who knows what Pencil's weakness is? But whatever that weakness turns out to be, we'll use it to stop it. So, we better be prepared for anything. Come on— follow me!"

Pencilmate and his friends, with Mini-

Pencilmate holding on to his new winged horse toy, ran into his bedroom and took a look at all his stuff. And there was a LOT of stuff to look at. First, there was a big bookcase full of books. Then, there was a stack of pillows piled up against the bookcase. And next to that was a large box labeled "Science Equipment for Making Science." On top of that box was another smaller box with a sticker that said "Very Important Thing Inside."

Also, the room was positively littered with toys. Spaceships, monsters, games . . . you name it, Pencilmate had it.

"So what should we take?" Pencilmiss said, looking at the vast assortment of stuff.

"Everything!" Pencilmate said. "Because who knows what we'll need or when we'll need it?"

"Okay," Pencilmiss replied. "But what are we going to use to carry *everything*?"

Pencilmate thought about that for a few seconds, scratching his chin. Pencilmiss thought about Pencilmate thinking, while Big Guy thought about eating more cereal, and Mini-Pencilmate thought about winged toy horses.

"I dunno," Pencilmate said at last. "Maybe . . ."

But before Pencilmate could say another word, Pencil appeared above them and drew a rather large suitcase that rested on top of Pencilmate's bed.

"Oh, well, there you go," Pencilmiss said, pointing at the suitcase.

"No!" Pencilmate warned. He had been burned by Pencil so many times before. He just knew it had to be some kind of trick. "Pencil made that suitcase! You know we can't trust that wretched writing implement!"

But Big Guy had no idea what a "wretched writing implement" was. He didn't know that

Pencilmate was talking about Pencil. All Big Guy saw was a really big suitcase and a roomful of stuff. So, wanting to be helpful, he picked up a bunch of that stuff and dumped it right inside the suitcase! First up was the big stack of pillows. Somehow, impossibly, they all fit inside!

"Huh," Pencilmiss said as she then watched Big Guy put the entire bookcase, books and all, into the suitcase.

They fit, too.

"You don't see that every day," she said.

Big Guy kept picking up stuff and putting it into the suitcase until the entire contents of Pencilmate's room were safely inside.

"I don't believe it," Pencilmate said, still suspicious. "What's the catch? Why would Pencil suddenly be so helpful when we're trying to stop it?"

Pencilmate leaned over, scratching his

head as he looked inside the suitcase that was somehow bigger on the inside than it was on the outside. He thought he could see the bookcase and the books far below him. It looked like they were falling!

Without warning, Pencil reappeared and bumped Pencilmate from behind with its eraser!

"Oof!" Pencilmate exclaimed as he fell inside the suitcase!

"Pencilmate!" Pencilmiss shouted as she reached a hand inside the suitcase, trying to grab her friend. But he was falling fast and far below her.

"We've got to save him!" Pencilmiss declared bravely.

She looked at Big Guy, who still had some cereal stuck to his face.

"I'm in," he said.

"But how?" Pencilmiss said. Then she turned to look at Mini-Pencilmate, who was playing with the big toy horse. The big toy horse with WINGS.

"I think we're about to do something really dangerous," Pencilmiss said.

Taking ahold of Big Guy and Mini-Pencilmate with his toy horse, Pencilmiss dove headfirst into the suitcase . . . and adventure!

CHAPTER FOUR

For about the first ten minutes, all Pencilmate could do was scream. There he was, falling, falling—*FALLING!*—through the suitcase into which Pencil had pushed him. And all around him was the stuff from his room. Everything that Big Guy had thrown into the suitcase was there, from the pillows to the bookcases, toys, the box with science stuff, and all his games.

But after about ten minutes of nonstop falling, Pencilmate calmed down a bit, because it seemed like the only thing that was happening was falling!

"To be honest, this kind of feels like flying,"

Pencilmate said to himself. "And anyway, wherever I'm going, at least I'll have my stuff, eventually."

So Pencilmate just enjoyed falling until another thought occurred to him. Sooner or later, he would come to the bottom of the giant suitcase. And if he hit the ground, he'd go *SPLAT!*, and the last thing he wanted was to be squashed flat like a Pencilmate pancake!

"Okay, changing my mind about the whole 'this kind of feels like flying' thing," Pencilmate said.

Then he shouted, "Help! Help! Help!"

As he fell, he noticed a book falling out of a nearby bookcase. The title was *How to Not Get Pushed Into a Seemingly Bottomless Suitcase.*

Pencilmate grumbled.

Then strangely enough, as if his cry for

help had been heard, Pencilmate saw something hurtling toward him.

It was . . . Pencil!

"Nope!" Pencilmate said flatly. "Go away! Whatever you're selling, I'm not buying!"

Pencil said nothing, of course. But it did suddenly start to sketch something on Pencilmate's back.

"What are you doing?" Pencilmate asked in a panicky voice. "You're not drawing an anvil, are you? Or an elephant? A grand piano?"

Pencil waggled back and forth as if to say, "No."

"Whew," Pencilmate said. "Because those are three things I do NOT need right now."

Then a couple of seconds later, Pencilmate felt straps attached to something like a backpack wrap around his body.

"Wait, that's not a backpack!" Pencilmate

said. "That's a parachute!"

Pencil then nodded as if to say, "Yes!"

"I suppose I should say, 'Thank you,'"
Pencilmate said, and Pencil nodded again. "But
the thing is, I don't trust you! I want to believe
there's a parachute in there, but how can I be
sure?"

Even as Pencilmate asked the question, he
realized the answer. There was no way he could
be sure. Pencil almost always did something to
mess with him.

But if there was even a slim chance that
Pencil was trying to help him, shouldn't he take
it? The alternative to trying the parachute was
to go *SPLAT!* at the bottom of the suitcase, and
that didn't sound so great.

Pencilmate took a deep breath and pulled the
cord on the parachute just as Pencil disappeared.

He expected, or at least hoped, to see the

big silk parachute billow out from the backpack, slowing his descent until Pencilmate touched down at the bottom.

Instead, this is what happened:

That's right; there was no parachute inside—
only Granny!

"Granny!" Pencilmate shouted. "What were
you doing in there?"

"Sleeping!" Granny said, rubbing her tired
eyes.

"No, I mean, how did you GET in there?"
Pencilmate asked.

"It's a funny story," Granny said. "I was at
home, taking a nap after talking to my neighbor
Gladys—you know Gladys, don't you? Her nephew
is a donkey named Bernard, who wants to be
a deep-sea diver but is allergic to the ocean.
Anyway, I drifted off to sleep and I was having a
nice dream about peas when suddenly the next
thing I know, I'm popping out of your backpack!"

"That's not my backpack," Pencilmate
corrected Granny. "It's supposed to be a
parachute!"

"Well, I'm not one to criticize, but it's a lousy parachute," Granny said. "I mean, all it had inside was me, and I'm hardly what you'd call a parachute."

Pencilmate couldn't believe the kind of day he was having. It started out bad enough, but then it just kept on getting worse and worse!

And speaking of worse, this seems like a good (or bad?) time to mention that the bottom of the suitcase, the one that Pencilmate was so worried about hitting?

Yeah, that was coming up.

"The bottom!" Pencilmate shouted as he held tight onto Granny. "We're going to go *SPA-DOINK!*"

"Oh, then I better take a nap first," Granny said, and she went back to sleep.

The bottom of the suitcase was rapidly approaching. Pencilmate saw the complete contents of his bedroom strewn about.

Things were not looking good!

"Pencilmate!"

At first, Pencilmate thought that maybe he was talking to himself without realizing it. But then he realized it didn't sound like his voice, and Pencilmate didn't do impressions.

Looking up, he saw Pencilmiss! And Big Guy! And Mini-Pencilmate, too! They were all sitting on the back of an absolutely huge toy Pegasus that Pencilmate instantly recognized as the Free Toy Surprise inside the gigantic box of Collect All the Winged Horses cereal!

But Big Guy faced the other way, looking at the horse's tail. Pencilmate noticed that Big Guy kept pressing a big button on the toy horse's back over and over and over again. The button was making the Pegasus's wings flap furiously!

"It has flapping-wing action," Big Guy announced proudly. "We're flying."

"More like controlled falling," Pencilmiss said. "But close enough!"

Then the Pegasus flew close to Pencilmate, and Pencilmiss grabbed his arm, pulling him atop the horse!

"Don't forget Granny!" Pencilmate said.

Pencilmiss reached out and took hold of the snoring Granny.

"Granny?" Pencilmiss said. "What's SHE doing here?"

"Sleeping," Pencilmate replied.

Before our friends could continue their cheerful reunion, however, Pencilmiss noticed an immediate problem.

"We're too heavy!" Pencilmiss said. "With you and Granny on the horse, now we're REALLY falling instead of flying! Big Guy, push that button faster!"

"Can do," Big Guy said, and he pushed the

button on the back of the toy horse faster than anyone in the history of pushing buttons on the back of toy horses had ever pushed a button before.*

FLAPPITY-FLAP-FLAP-FLAP went the horse, its wings beating like a bat stuck on fast-forward.

And you know what? It was working!

The bottom of the suitcase with all of Pencilmate's stuff wasn't coming up quite so quickly anymore, and it looked like Pencilmiss was going to be able to bring the Pegasus in for a soft landing!

At least, she *would* have been able to do that—if Pencil hadn't suddenly appeared below and started to scribble . . .

*Just so you know, that's pretty fast.

CHAPTER FIVE

"Hey, guys?" Pencilmiss said as the winged horse set down. "We're on the Moon."

And you know what? They WERE on the Moon! That's because, at the last possible second, Pencil drew a brand-new setting. The inside of the suitcase with all of Pencilmate's stuff was now gone. And in its place was a barren, slightly green lunar landscape. They all jumped off the winged horse to explore their new surroundings.

"Also, we're wearing astronaut suits," Pencilmate pointed out, noticing his backpack was gone.

And you know what? They WERE wearing astronaut suits! That's because—even though it liked to take pokes at Pencilmate and his pals—Pencil wasn't completely heartless. Besides, if Pencilmate and his friends didn't survive on the surface of the Moon, then who would Pencil have to push around? Nobody? Where's the fun in that?

Pencilmate sighed. He saw nothing around him but a sea of green, and he thought that was a little odd.

"What gives?" Pencilmate said. "I thought the Moon was supposed to be gray."

Big Guy scratched the top of his head, except he was wearing a helmet, so he scratched the top of that instead.

"I'm thinking," Big Guy said. Then he fell over, because that's what happened whenever Big Guy tried to think.

Because the gravity on the Moon wasn't as strong as it was on Earth, Big Guy fell to the ground slowly. He landed softly, with a couple of bounces.

Big Guy looked at the green surface of the Moon, then his eyes went wide.

"Yum," he said. "Yum, yum, yum!"

"Uh-oh," Pencilmate said. "I think Big Guy's got Moon Sickness."

"What's Moon Sickness?" Pencilmiss asked.

"I don't know, but I think he's got it," Pencilmate replied.

Then Big Guy scooped up a big handful of green stuff from the Moon's surface. He opened the visor on his astronaut helmet and shoved the big glob of green into his mouth. And he chewed, and it sounded like *CHOMP GLOMP GLUMP CHOMP CHOMP!*

"What are you doing?" Pencilmiss said,

shaking Big Guy. "This is the Moon! You can't just open your helmet like that! And you also can't eat the Moon!"

"But it is cheese," Big Guy said, a blissful look on his face.

This piqued Mini-Pencilmate's interest, and he took off his helmet.

"Mini-Pencilmate, no!" Pencilmiss said, but it was already too late.

Mini-Pencilmate had already grabbed some of the Moon and stuck it in his mouth.

CHOMP GLOMP CLUMP CHOMP CHOMP!

Pencilmate watched his friends, then took a handful of the Moon, too. Cautiously, he opened the visor on his helmet and sniffed the green stuff.

"Well, whaddya know," Pencilmate said. "It *is* cheese! Also, we can breathe on the Moon, apparently."

Pencilmiss took off her helmet and rolled her eyes. "Then what's the point of the spacesuits?" she asked.

That's a great question, Pencilmiss. We may never know!

"Free cheese," Big Guy said, his mouth overflowing with cheesy goodness. "This is the best day ever."

"I don't know about best day ever,"

Pencilmate said. "I mean, I'm happy for you and your cheese. But we're stuck on the Moon. How are we supposed to get home? And how are we going to find out Pencil's weakness?!?"

Pencilmiss nodded and said, "Maybe Granny will have some ideas."

But when she looked at Granny, Pencilmiss was surprised to see that she was still asleep in her spacesuit, standing straight up. She took off her helmet, and the sound of Granny's loud snoring filled the air.

"Granny, wake up!" Pencilmiss said, shaking her.

"Huh, what?" Granny said, coming out of her sleep. "Is it my birthday? An all-expenses-paid trip to the Moon? You shouldn't have."

"It isn't, and we didn't," Pencilmate said. "Pencil put us here! And we gotta get back home so we can stop that pest!"

"Oh, well, if it isn't an all-expenses-paid trip for my birthday, I don't want to be on the Moon," Granny grumbled. "That Pencil. Ugh. It's the worst. Always mucking things up for the rest of us."

"Exactly!" Pencilmate said. "Granny gets it! So, what are we gonna do?"

Big Guy, who was still lying down on the Moon eating cheese, said, "I have an idea."

"Really?" Pencilmiss asked. "And what is it?"

"Eat more cheese," Big Guy said. "I am so good at it."

"I don't think eating cheese is going to help us," Pencilmiss said. "But maybe we could use the cheese somehow."

"I got it!" Pencilmate said. "Why don't we make a spaceship out of cheese? Then we could just fly back home and find Pencil's weakness!"

"That," Big Guy said, "is not as good an idea as eating cheese."

But Pencilmiss and Granny were totally on board with the plan. At once, they started scooping up big hunks of cheese from the Moon's surface. With help from Mini-Pencilmate, who turned out to be really good at squishing cheese together so it looked like a spaceship, the friends formed their interstellar vehicle.

Also, Big Guy ate some more cheese.

After a while, the spaceship was really starting to take shape.

"Y'know," Pencilmate said, "I think this is going to work! Look out, Pencil—here we come!"

Unfortunately, and unknown to Pencilmate and the others, Pencil had been hovering around, peering over the edge of a nearby crater. It was watching them, curious to see what they would try to do.

And it decided that now—when they were so close to completing their spaceship, and their goal of returning home was just within reach—Pencil would mess with them again.

It popped out of the crater and drew a little monkey.

Granny was the first to notice what was going on.

"Hey," she said, slapping some cheese on the side of the spaceship. "I don't want to rain on anyone's parade, but Pencil's over there drawing a monkey."

Everyone except Big Guy (because: eating cheese) turned to look at the monkey. It was a very cute monkey, and the little fella smiled and waved at them.

"Seems harmless," Pencilmate said. "Which of course means that it isn't."

Pencil nodded, as it drew another monkey. Then another. And another.

The impish implement was now drawing with mesmerizing speed, making monkey after monkey. There was now an entire jumble of monkeys.

But these weren't ordinary monkeys.

No, they were Moon Monkeys!

"EEK EEK! OOK OOK!" the Moon Monkeys said in unison.

Then the little guys bounced across the Moon's surface, coming right for Pencilmate and his pals!

"I'm going to say in advance that I don't like Moon Monkeys," Pencilmate said.

"Agreed," Pencilmiss added.

The Moon Monkeys were all over them in seconds. Except the super-cute simians didn't seem particularly interested in Pencilmate,

Pencilmiss, Mini-Pencilmate, or Granny. They certainly weren't interested in Big Guy, who was still just lying there eating cheese.

No, the hungry Moon Monkeys were interested in the cheese itself—specifically, the spaceship that Pencilmate and his friends had been making!

"Hey! Get away from our ship, Moon Monkeys!" Pencilmate said, swatting at the little mischief-makers.

"EEK! OOK!" a Moon Monkey shouted at Pencilmate as it grabbed a hunk of cheese off the spaceship and stuffed it in its mouth.

"Oh come on, that's no *gouda*!" Pencilmate said.

Pencilmiss just looked at him and said, "How can you make cheese puns at a time like this?"

"*Brie*-lieve me, it's not easy," Pencilmate replied.

"I think," Big Guy said, "those Moon Monkeys are just as hungry as I am."

As a couple of Moon Monkeys jumped on top of Granny's head, she said, "I think these Moon Monkeys better get off my head, or there's gonna be trouble. Granny trouble."

Everyone gasped, because if there's one thing you don't want, it's Granny trouble.

Well, the Moon Monkeys didn't gasp. But that's only because they were too busy eating cheese.

Same with Big Guy; he didn't gasp, either.

Granny grabbed the two Moon Monkeys by their feet and swung them around. Then she let go, and the Moon Monkeys sailed through the air slowly, eventually landing softly on the Moon's cheesy surface.

The two Moon Monkeys looked at each other, then at the ground, and started to scoop up cheese and eat it.

And this gave Pencilmate a big idea.

"Those Moon Monkeys don't want to destroy our ship," Pencilmate whispered to Pencilmiss. "They're just hungry! So what if we give them something else to eat?"

"Like what?" Pencilmiss asked. "It's not like we brought any bananas with us!"

But then she smiled. So did Pencilmate.

"No," Pencilmate said. "But I know someone who can help."

Then, as more Moon Monkeys approached the ship, and Pencil watched from behind, Pencilmate shouted, "If only we had some bananas that we could use to distract the Moon Monkeys!"

"Pencilmate, no!" Pencilmiss yelled. "Don't wish for bananas! Bananas are the LAST thing we need right now! They could—*GASP!*—destroy us!"

It goes without saying that Pencil simply could not help itself. Now all it wanted to do was draw a colossal bunch of bananas and sit back and watch as the Moon Monkeys used the fruit to cause absolute mayhem.

As soon as Pencil drew the bananas, Pencilmiss seized the opportunity to take them and hurl them at the hungry Moon Monkeys.

Instantly, their eyes lit up. An eager Moon Monkey picked up one of the bananas and shoved it in their mouth without even peeling it.

"Oh my gosh!" the Moon Monkey said, surprising everyone. "This is so good! Dig in, everybody! We finally got something else to eat besides cheese!"

"Wait, you can talk?!?" Pencilmate said.

"Sure we can talk," the Moon Monkey said as it took another banana. "When we have something worth saying."

Soon, all the Moon Monkeys swarmed around the bananas, eating them like—well, like monkeys.

Meanwhile, Pencil was positively fuming! It wasn't used to having its own powers turned against it. And now it was mad!

But in the confusion of Moon Monkeys eating bananas, Pencilmate and his friends managed to complete their cheese spaceship.

And before Pencil could draw anything else that might stop them, Pencilmate, Pencilmiss, Mini-Pencilmate, Granny, and Big Guy (who was somehow still eating cheese) escaped.

CHAPTER SIX

The cheese spaceship turned out to be superfast, and before they knew it, Pencilmate and his friends were entering Earth's atmosphere.

"I can see my backyard!" Pencilmate shouted as the spaceship soared through the sky toward his home.

"I can see my hands!" Big Guy said excitedly.

"*Everyone* can see your hands," Pencilmiss said.

"All right," Pencilmate said. "We'll be landing in a minute. Let's hit the air brakes."

But Pencilmiss was already at the controls.

"I already hit the air brakes," she said.

"We're not slowing down! We're going to crash!"

Even with the air brakes on, the spaceship plummeted toward Pencilmate's backyard.

"Brace yourselves, everyone!" Pencilmate said.

The spaceship was coming in hot and slammed into the grass with a loud *WHOMP!*

Then things took a turn for the weird.

They got weird because Pencil was already there, waiting for Pencilmate and his pals. Pencil scribbled all over the backyard, and then suddenly, everything (including this very page) tilted on its side! The ground shifted up, and the spaceship fell toward the bottom as Pencilmate and his friends spilled out of the craft.

"This is a catastrophe!" Pencilmate said. "A CATASTROPHE, I tell you!"

Then Pencil started to scribble something else. Instantly, a clowder of super-cute cats appeared, meowing and purring!

"Hey, look," Big Guy said. "Cats!"

"Cats, huh," Granny said. "Time to make some kitty sweaters."

Then she whipped out some yarn and knitting needles from her pocket and started to make a sweater.

"How can you knit sweaters at a time like this?!?" Pencilmiss asked.

"Well, I don't want the kitties to catch a cold," Granny explained.

As everyone continued to fall, Pencilmate swore that he could hear Pencil laughing.

Except . . . it wasn't the sound of Pencil laughing. It was just the meowing and purring of the super-cute cats.

Then, just as quickly as the weirdness started, Pencilmate and his friends landed on a big stack of paper!

"Oof!" Pencilmate said, hitting the paper

hard as he watched Big Guy catch Mini-Pencilmate. Meanwhile, Granny had not only knitted a kitten sweater but also managed to knit a parachute that she used to bring herself and Pencilmiss to safety. (Don't worry about the cats—they all landed on their feet.)

"Wait, how did you knit a complete sweater AND a parachute so fast?" Pencilmiss wondered.

"I'm not *knit*-ting around when it comes to sweaters!" Granny said with a smile, pocketing her knitting needles.

Pencilmate stood up, rubbing his head.

"Where are we?" he asked.

He had never seen anything like it before! Pencilmate glanced at the stack of blank white paper, the pages positively huge compared to him and his friends. But there were other objects as well. What appeared to be giant pens and pencils (but not Pencil) sat on a flat wooden surface, along with a big pink eraser and a huge ruler.

"This kind of looks like an artist's desk," Pencilmiss suggested.

"No," Pencilmate said quickly, "but it DOES kind of look like an ARTIST'S desk!"

Pencilmiss sighed and rolled her eyes.

"Somehow, this is even weirder than being on the Moon," Granny said.

By now, she had managed to knit sweaters for each one of the meowing cats that surrounded them.

"Boy, you're fast," Big Guy said as he and Mini-Pencilmate began to pet as many cats as they possibly could.

But Pencilmate looked gloomier than ever.

"We are in a pickle," he said.

"No we're not," Big Guy protested. "Believe me, I'd know if I was in a pickle."

BIG GUY

BIG GUY IN A PICKLE

"No, not that kind of pickle," Pencilmate said.
"We're in a mess, I mean! Not only do we still
have to find Pencil's weakness and stop it from
messing with us anymore, but we also need to
find a way back home."

"We escaped from the Moon, didn't we?"
Pencilmiss said.

"But that was different," Pencilmate said.
"Getting back from the Moon was easy. Just build
a spaceship and zoom! But this . . . we don't even

know where we are! So how can we find our way home?"

While all this was going on, a pencil stirred. Not just any pencil, either. It was Pencil! It was there, watching the whole thing. And it decided that staring at Pencilmate and his friends moping and whining about getting home was pretty boring.

So, it was time to stir things up.

Pencilmate gasped when he noticed Pencil fly up into the air and quickly write a note on a piece of paper.

The note said,

You are so boring! So, so boring!
So now I am going to use my
ultimate weapon, you know,
to keep things interesting!

"Hey, who are you calling 'boring'?" Granny

said in an angry voice. "I'm the most interesting person here!"

"That's probably true," Big Guy offered.

But words weren't going to stop Pencil. It flipped around, so the eraser on its other end faced Pencilmate and his pals.

"Not the eraser!" Pencilmate said. "It's gonna wipe us out! How can we defend ourselves against that?!?"

"I got one word for you, kid," Granny said. Then she picked up the giant ruler and wielded it like a spear. "Supplies!"

As Pencil moved in to erase Mini-Pencilmate first, Granny swung the ruler.

THWACK!

She smacked Pencil, and the awful implement went flying.

"Yes, Granny!" Pencilmiss shouted. Then she picked up a pen. As Pencil recovered, she pressed a button on the pen, and ink squirted out.

SPLOOSH!

Pencil was now covered in ink.

Then Pencilmate and Big Guy looked at each other as an angry Pencil began bouncing their way.

They pushed a group of pencils toward their foe, and they rolled along the wooden surface, tripping up Pencil!

This gave Granny time to fold a paper airplane. She hurled it at her enemy, and the paper airplane bonked Pencil right in the lead.

Pencil wrote a little note that said, "OUCH!"

Now Pencil was absolutely steaming. It couldn't get close enough to Pencilmate and the others to use its eraser. But it still had more tricks up its sleeves, even though it didn't have any sleeves, because pencils don't wear shirts.

It started to scribble once more.

"What's Pencil doing?" Pencilmate asked.

"Looks like the backstroke," Big Guy said.

"Big Guy, do you see a pool?" Pencilmiss asked. "Pencil's not swimming."

"Oh," Big Guy replied. "I have trouble telling the difference between swimming and drawing."

But it soon became apparent what Pencil was up to. Sketching furiously, Pencil created an entire army of Moon Monkeys. Not only that, but it also drew the very same sea monster that chased Pencilmate at the beginning of this very book!

"EEK! OOK!" cried the Moon Monkeys.

"SEA MONSTER NOISES!" screamed the sea monster.

"This looks like the end," Pencilmate gulped. "At least I'm with my friends."

"Speak for yourself," Granny said.

"Wait!" Pencilmiss shouted. "Look!"

Just as the Moon Monkeys were about to attack, they saw the super-cute cats in their super-cute sweaters. Little hearts popped up in their Moon Monkey eyes, and they began cuddling their new feline friends!

"Okay, that's one enemy down," Pencilmiss said. "But we still have that sea monster to deal with. And then there's Pencil!"

Things were slightly better but still not looking good. Slowly, an idea began to form in Pencilmate's brain, right next to an idea he had about getting ice cream after all this was done.

"Pencil's ultimate weapon is its eraser," Pencilmate said. "Maybe . . . maybe it's also Pencil's weakness!"

"Oh, I get it!" Pencilmiss said. "We can use its own weapon against it!"

"And there's a big eraser right over there!"

Pencilmate said, pointing at the other side of the desk. "So here's what we're gonna do . . ."

(This is the part of the book where the heroes whisper and make their plan.)

But it's impolite to eavesdrop, and besides, you want it to be a surprise, don't you? That's what we thought.

As Pencilmate and Pencilmiss made a break for the big eraser, Granny, Big Guy, and Mini-Pencilmate distracted the sea monster by singing a sea shanty. "Shanty" is another word for "song," which makes you wonder why we didn't just say that in the first place. They didn't have to distract the Moon Monkeys, as the cats already did that job for them.

"Almost there!" Pencilmate said.

But just as they were about to reach the big eraser, they heard the sea monster scream, "BOO! BOOOOOOOO!"

"Oh no!" Pencilmiss said. "The sea monster hates sea shanties!"

The sea monster reared up and wrapped its long neck around Granny, Big Guy, and Mini-Pencilmate.

They were now the prisoners of Pencil!

CHAPTER SEVEN

With his friends now captured by his worst enemy, Pencilmate could only stand next to Pencilmiss and watch as Pencil hastily wrote another note. This one said,

> I know what you're planning,
> so don't even think about it!
> I'll erase your friends unless
> you give me that big eraser
> over there.

"I'll say this for Pencil," Pencilmate said. "It sure can write fast."

"I know, right?" Pencilmiss replied.

"So, what do you think we should do?" Pencilmate asked his friend.

"I think we should do as it says," Pencilmiss said with a grin.

Pencilmate immediately picked up on what Pencilmiss was thinking. He turned toward Pencil and smiled the widest smile he had ever smiled in his life.

"Of *course* we'll give it to you!" Pencilmate said.

Suddenly, Pencilmate and Pencilmiss grabbed the big eraser and charged straight at Pencil!

It was clear just by looking at it that Pencil hadn't counted on the courage of Pencilmate and Pencilmiss. Pencil started to shake like it was panicking! It began bouncing on its eraser, trying to escape. But it bonked right into the sea monster!

THOOMP!

Stunned, the sea monster let go of Granny, Big Guy, and Mini-Pencilmate. Then it stumbled into one of the Moon Monkeys, who was eating bananas.

ZOOMP!

The Moon Monkey fell over into another Moon Monkey eating bananas right next to them. Then THAT Moon Monkey hit the next one and so on, down the line, until all the Moon Monkeys had fallen over like dominoes!

Now free, Granny, Big Guy, and Mini-Pencilmate joined Pencilmate and Pencilmiss.

"C'mon, guys!" Pencilmate shouted. "Let's give Pencil a taste of its own medicine!"

With the big eraser in their hands, the group went after Pencil. The writing implement bounced around all over the desk, trying to get away. But there was no exit!

At last, Pencilmate and his friends backed Pencil into a corner.

Well, not a corner, exactly.

They backed it up against . . . a pencil sharpener!

"You've got nowhere to go, Pencil!" Pencilmate said. "You're between a rock and a hard place!"

"More like an eraser and a pencil sharpener," Granny said. "But it's the same idea, I suppose."

"You know what I wish?" Big Guy said.

"Um, kinda busy now, Big Guy," Pencilmiss said. "But what do you wish?"

"I wish we had more of that Moon cheese," Big Guy said, rubbing his tummy.

Everyone looked at Big Guy, including Pencil, as if to say, "Really? At a time like this?"

"We'll come back to that," Pencilmate said. "But now, Pencil, what's it gonna be? Do we erase you from existence?"

Mini-Pencilmate gasped!

"Or," Pencilmate continued, "do we put you in that pencil sharpener and grind you away into nothingness?"

Mini-Pencilmate gasped again!

Pencil wobbled back and forth as if trying to figure out what to do. It tried to make a break for it, but Pencilmate and his friends blocked Pencil's path with the big eraser.

"Boy, how I've wished for this moment!" Pencilmate said. "You're always causing trouble for us. So this is what it feels like to finally have the upper hand!"

Pencilmate lunged forward slightly, the eraser coming dangerously close to Pencil. He watched as his foe trembled. It wasn't even trying to escape anymore.

And then something very strange happened.

Pencilmate started to feel . . . bad for Pencil!

"It's . . . it's afraid," Pencilmate said softly. "Pencil really is afraid."

"Great! Let's get rid of it and go home," Granny said. "Somewhere, there's a grilled cheese sandwich with my name on it."

"We . . . we can't," Pencilmiss said.

"You're right," Pencilmate agreed. "If we try to erase Pencil, or sharpen it, or whatever, then we'll be just as bad. Nothing but bullies!"

"But we also can't just do nothing," Pencilmiss said. "Otherwise, Pencil's going to keep on messing with you. With us! Forever!"

So Pencilmate thought for a moment, rubbing his chin. The whole time, Pencil watched him, trembling and waiting for Pencilmate to speak.

Finally, Pencilmate said, "Okay, Pencil. I'm willing to make you a deal. But you have to stick to it, okay?"

Pencil nodded vigorously as if to say, "Yes! Anything! As long as you don't sharpen me or erase me, because either of those options really stinks!"

"All right, then. We agree to let you go unharmed," Pencilmate said. "And in return, YOU promise not to mess with us anymore."

Quiet filled the air as Pencil began to scribble something on a scrap of paper. The note said,

Define "mess with."

Big Guy wasn't playing, so he picked up the big eraser all by himself and came at Pencil!

This prompted Pencil to hastily write,

Okay, okay, I promise!!

"I think you can back down now, Big Guy," Pencilmate said. "We have a truce. Right, Pencil?"

Pencil nodded.

"Well," Pencilmiss said, "now that we've solved this particular problem, how are we going to get back home?"

But Pencil had already thought about that. It wrote,

That's easy! Just watch!

Then Pencil started to draw, and a couple of seconds later, an elevator appeared on top of the desk.

"Wow, that really WAS easy," Pencilmiss said.

"You know, you're pretty resourceful,"

Pencilmate said, complimenting Pencil.

As the elevator doors opened, Pencilmate and his friends stepped inside along with Pencil.

But before the doors closed, the sea monster and the Moon Monkeys and the super-cute cats also piled in! Soon, there wasn't any space left at all, and everyone was crammed in like cereal in a box.

"I didn't realize they were gonna come with," Granny said, her face smooshed up against a Moon Monkey.

At last, the elevator doors closed.

When the elevator doors opened on Pencilmate's front lawn, Moon Monkeys and cats spilled out everywhere. By sheer coincidence, a banana delivery truck drove past, and the hungry Moon Monkeys chased after it. The cats, on the other hand, stayed close to Granny.

"Well, the problem of what we're going to do with the Moon Monkeys just solved itself," Pencilmate said.

The sea monster then looked at Pencilmate, giving him puppy-dog eyes.

"I know what you're trying to do," Pencilmate

said, "and it won't work! There's no way you're staying—"

But the sea monster just kept making their eyes bigger and bigger, and then they started to cry, and Pencilmate couldn't take it anymore.

"All right, all right, you can stay!" Pencilmate said. "But I get the bed."

Overjoyed, the sea monster raced into the house.

That left Pencilmate and his friends standing on the front lawn alone with Pencil.

"Well, I certainly hope you've learned your lesson," Pencilmate said.

Pencil nodded.

"I wonder what things will be like now that you won't be messing with us?" Pencilmiss wondered.

Then Pencil began to write something on

Pencilmate's driveway. It said,

Yeah, see . . . about that . . .
. . . when I promised not
to mess with you? I had
my fingers crossed.

Pencil bounced up and down on its eraser excitedly as Pencilmate and his friends looked on, their jaws dropping open.

"But you don't even HAVE fingers!" Pencilmate hollered just as Pencil disappeared.

"Well, that was fun," Granny said. "Now someone make me a grilled cheese sandwich before I become grumpy."

"You already ARE grumpy," Pencilmiss said.

"See how fast it happens?" Granny replied.

Pencilmiss turned to her friend and noticed that somehow, Pencilmate was actually smiling.

"Why do you look so happy?" Pencilmiss asked. "Your worst enemy just backed out of a promise never to mess with you. Pencil lied to you, to us!"

"I know," Pencilmate said. "But if I'm being honest, if we didn't have Pencil to deal with, what would we do all day?"

"Um, enjoy NOT being messed with?" Pencilmiss suggested.

"Yeah, but that would get tired real quick," Pencilmate said. "Anyway, Pencil should leave us alone for a little while at least. So why don't we go inside, I'll make everyone some grilled cheese sandwiches, and we can figure out what a sea monster likes to eat. Sound good?"

"I think we already established that a sea monster would like to eat US," Granny said.

"Hah! You crack me up, Granny!" Pencilmate said, slapping Granny on the back.

Then they all walked into Pencilmate's house for grilled cheese sandwiches and to try not getting eaten by a sea monster.